THE CELERY STALKS AT MIDNIGHT

THE
CELERY STALKS
AT MIDNIGHT

THE CELERY STALKS AT MIDNIGHT

JAMES HOWE

SCHOLASTIC INC.

New York Toronto London Auckland Sydney
Mexico City New Delhi Hong Kong Buenos Aires

ISBN 0-439-43183-2

12 11 10 9 8 7 6 5 4 3 2   2 3 4 5 6 7/0

Printed in the U.S.A.   40

First Scholastic printing, September 2002

Designed by Mary Ahern

To my father,

who raised me on a

diet of corn, ham,

and punster cheese.

Contents

[EDITOR'S NOTE]

HAVING BEEN in the publishing business for many years, there is little left to surprise me. I have, as Harold puts it in his new book, come to "expect the unexpected." So I wasn't surprised in the least to receive a phone call recently from a well-known literary agent asking me to take a look at a new client's book. Business as usual, I thought. Imagine my amazement upon receipt of the manuscript and following note to discover just *who* her new client was.

Dear Ed, (the author wrote familiarly)

I hope you won't think I've "gone Hollywood," but my friend Chester convinced me that with this, my third book, I should hire an agent. "After all," he counseled me, "who's going to handle all those requests that will undoubtedly pour in for your personal appearances on the **Today** *show,* *the* Tonight *show and* Animal Kingdom? *And who will watch over your editor to make sure he treats you with the respect due the most famous canine author since Erich Beagle?" I hope you will forgive the latter comment as I have had no complaints with your treatment of me thus far and anticipate only the best in our continued relationship.*

Nonetheless, I have engaged the services of a literary agent who will deliver these pages to you. For this and other services, I am sure she will be worth her weight in dog biscuits.

Once again, I do hope you will view publication of my work favorably.

> *Yours sincerely,*
> *Harold X.*

I gazed out the window next to my desk and watched a new skyscraper being erected nearby. There's no stopping progress, I mused. With a sigh, I turned my attention back to Harold's manuscript. I would miss his familiar bedraggled figure appearing unannounced at my door, his latest effort clenched between his teeth. To think that Harold, of all writers, should have hired an agent! It was with a heavy heart indeed that I began to read the manuscript entitled *The Celery Stalks at Midnight.*

But it was not long before I forgot everything save the harrowing story that unfolded in the pages therein. It is a story that dares to ask the question: When the moon is up and the night creatures begin to stir, who knows what evil lurks in the hearts of lettuce?

For the answer, read on.

THE CELERY STALKS AT MIDNIGHT

The Disappearance

IT WAS NOT a dark and stormy night. Indeed, there was nothing in the elements to fore-shadow the events that lay ahead.

Chester, Howie and I were gathered on the front porch for a bit of post-dinner snoozing. I was stretched out on my back, my paws dangling at my sides, thinking of nothing more than the meal I'd just eaten and the chocolate treat I hoped might still lie ahead. After all, it *was* Friday night, the one night of the week Toby was allowed to stay up to read as late as he wanted. And that meant snacks. Snacks to be shared with his old pal, Harold. That's me.

Chester, curled up on an open comic book nearby, purred contentedly. Only Howie, who was growling as he chewed vigorously on a rawhide bone, seemed unable to relax. But all that high-strung energy was natural, I suppose, considering he was still just a puppy.

"Boy, this is the life, huh, Uncle Harold?" Howie asked between growls.

"Mmph," I replied with as much vigor as I could muster. Which wasn't much. After all, I *wasn't* a puppy anymore and had used up most of my energy long ago. I listened to the sound of children playing down the block somewhere.

"There's nothing like hanging out on the porch after a good meal," Howie went on enthusiastically. He lifted his quivering nostrils to the air and sniffed rapidly.

"Ahhh! Smell that night air. Mmm, what's that? Somebody's having a . . . a what'd ya call it? What is it when they cook outside, Pop?"

Chester raised an eyelid. "A barbecue," he said with a yawn.

"Oh, yeah. Gee, I have so much to learn. But you and Uncle Harold have taught me a lot already." He gazed admiringly at Chester. "Thanks, Pop," he said.

Chester raised his other eyelid and shook his head. He turned his gaze from Howie to me.

"Why does the kid insist on calling me 'Pop'?" he asked. "I'm not his father. I'm not even a dog. If anyone around here should be his 'pop,' it should be you, Harold. Dogs of a feather should stick together and all that."

Howie chuckled. "That's a good one, Pop. 'Dogs of a feather . . . ' I'll have to remember that one."

I didn't even attempt to answer Chester's question. After all, Chester, who doesn't hold dogs in particularly high regard, did seem an odd choice of a father figure for a young pup. But Howie, who had recently come to live with us, had formed his attachment right away, and there was no breaking him of it now.

"Too bad the rabbit can't come out here, too," Howie went on with a nod toward the living room. "It's not fair, his having to be cooped up inside that cage all the time."

"I'm afraid that's a rabbit's fate," I said. "At least for a domesticated one. Though I must agree with you, Howie; I feel sorry for Bunnicula, too."

"Save your sympathy," Chester muttered. "Bunnicula is no ordinary rabbit. If he ever got out . . . and let's not forget that once upon a time he did, Harold . . . he'd only stir up trouble."

"Are you still convinced—" I started to say, but stopped myself, not wanting to alarm young Howie with Chester's theories of Bunnicula's true identity.

Chester looked mildly surprised. "Of course, I am," he replied. "Can there be any doubt? You saw the evidence yourself, Harold."

Howie looked back and forth from Chester to

me. "What are you two talking about?" he asked.

"Oh, nothing. Nothing." I thought of the cuddly little bunny-rabbit who'd become my friend, of the hours we'd spent snuggling in front of crackling fires on cold winter nights, of the time I'd saved him from Chester's attempt to starve him to death.

"That rabbit is a vampire," Chester said matter-of-factly.

Howie's head jerked up. The rawhide bone tumbled down the front steps. "What? A vampire?" He gasped. Then, after a moment's reflection, he asked, "What's a vampire?"

I felt obliged to step in and save Howie from the seamier facts of life.

"A vampire," I explained, "is the person who calls the rules during a baseball game."

"Don't confuse the kid," Chester said, bathing a paw. "And don't be such a Pollyanna." Turning to Howie, he said, "A vampire is a creature, once dead, who sucks the blood out of other living beings in order to live."

Howie's eyes widened in amazement.

"Wh . . . wh . . . what?" he stammered.

"So far, our friend Bunnicula hasn't attacked people," Chester went on calmly, "or cats or dogs for that matter. But he has drained the juices out of vegetables, turning them ghostly white. He came to live with us when our family . . . "

"One night the Monroes went to the movies," I said, picking up the story, "and found Bunnicula lying in a dirt-filled box on one of the seats."

"Don't forget which movie," Chester interjected.

"*Dracula,*" I conceded, "but that doesn't mean—"

"Nonsense. In this case, everything means something. Don't you think it's significant that shortly after Bunnicula's arrival the vegetables in the kitchen started turning white? And wasn't it strange that they did so during the night, the only time Bunnicula wasn't asleep? Wasn't it stranger still that he could get out of his cage by his own powers? Without even undoing the lock? And what about those marks found in the drained vegetables? Two tiny holes that matched up perfectly with the rabbit's oddly-spaced teeth . . . or should I say, fangs?"

"I know, I know," I said impatiently. "We've been through all this before. But I'm still not convinced—"

"Nothing will ever convince you, Harold. I wouldn't be surprised if that bunny's got you in his powers. Listen, Howie . . . "

"Yes, Pop?"

Chester rolled his eyes and went on. "You can't listen to Harold on this one. He's too much of a goody-two-shoes. And the Monroes . . . well, what can I say? People are, alas, people, and, as such, woefully in the dark much of the time. They never had a clue what was going on. I was on the verge of destroying the vampire bunny once and for all, saving this town and all its inhabitants from his evil clutches, when the Monroes whisked him off to the vet and got him put on a liquid diet. Since then, he's had no need to suck the juices out of vegetables. A blender does all the work for him. Modern technology has once again saved the day. But . . . " and here Chester furrowed his brow ominously, "you can take the rabbit out of the vampire, but you can't take the vampire out of the rabbit."

"Huh?" I inquired.

"I don't get it," Howie said, scratching behind his ear with his back paw.

"You can take the—oh, never mind. What I'm trying to say is that I still believe if, for any reason, Bunnicula were deprived of his liquified vegetables, or had the opportunity to run away, he'd be back to his old tricks in no time."

Howie was so aroused by Chester's story he was panting slightly. "Wow," he said, trying to catch his breath, "and all this time I thought he was just a nice little bunny."

"He *is* a nice little bunny," I asserted, feeling the need to defend my friend. "Don't listen to Chester."

"Don't listen to Harold."

"Chester," I said.

"Harold."

"Pop, Uncle Harold," Howie barked. "Stop arguing. You're confusing me. I think I'd better run out and chase a car to clear my mind. Excuse me."

Howie started down the steps when Mrs. Monroe appeared at the door.

"Hello, boys," she said warmly. "I was wondering where you'd disappeared to. Howie, come back here. I've told you not to run out into the street."

"Rats," Howie muttered under his breath. He turned his face up toward the door and began whimpering.

"Now, that won't do you any good. Come on," she said, "it's getting late. Time to come in for the night. We're all going to bed."

Howie and I, being the obedient dog-types that we are, started for the door. Chester, a cat, lingered on his comic book, looking up at Mrs. Monroe with singular disinterest. She went over and picked him up. "Let's go, you little cutie," she cooed. "Sleepy-time."

Chester grimaced. " 'Little cutie,' 'sleepy-time,' good grief," I heard him mumble.

We entered the living room to find Toby and

Pete, the Monroes' two sons, staring into the television set as if they'd been hypnotized. I went over to Toby's side to see what it was all about.

"Gotcha!" Toby yelled suddenly, making me jump.

Pete bounced and twitched all over the floor as he frantically turned some dials back and forth and little blobs of light darted all over the screen. Weird noises—squawks and beeps and screeches—emanated from inside the television.

"I think our TV's possessed," I whispered to Chester, who'd jumped down from Mrs. Monroe's arms to join us.

"Don't panic, Harold," he reassured me. "I'll take care of it."

Slowly, he skulked across the floor, his eyes never straying from the flecks of light that dashed about maniacally on the screen. Every time two of them collided, another hideous screech was heard. When that happened, Chester's head jerked, his eyes widened, and a little more hair shot up along his back.

Suddenly, he pounced. With his paws racing

madly across the screen, he tried to catch the screaming specks of light.

"Chester!" Pete yelled. "Get out of the way."

"Yeah, Chester," Toby joined in. "Come on, you're ruining the game!" I was a little surprised at Toby, who was usually more patient than his brother. He now seemed as transformed as Pete by this strange new enterprise of theirs.

"All right, boys," Mrs. Monroe said, touching them lightly on the tops of their heads, "that's enough Star-Thrower for tonight."

"Star-*Eater*, Mom!"

"Yeah, Mom. Jeez."

"Star-Thrower, Star-Eater, whatever. It's time to call it quits and get to bed. Toby, you want time to sit up and read, don't you?"

"Yeah, I guess," Toby said. "Chester!" Chester was still busy trying to catch the elusive stars. "Just one more game, Mom. Okay?"

"No, it's not okay. Robert."

Mr. Monroe put down the book he was reading in a chair nearby. "You boys have a big day to-morrow," he said. "I think you'd better get some sleep. You heard your mother—no more Star-Catcher."

"Star-Eater, dear," Mrs. Monroe said. "I'm going to count to three. One, two . . . "

"Okay, okay," Pete said, and with a click the stars disappeared from the television sky. Chester, his front paws still stretched out on the screen, looked dazed.

"Everybody to bed. Now."

"Okay, we're going." The boys started up the stairs.

I planned to follow when suddenly I noticed Howie run up to Chester and whisper excitedly.

"Pop! Pop!"

Chester kept blinking his eyes at the television as if trying to figure out what had happened.

"What, kid?"

"Pop, what you said about Bunnicula. Your warning . . . "

"What about it?"

I glanced over to the rabbit's cage.

"Chester!" I gasped.

Chester dropped down and looked at us.

"What's the matter with you two?"

Howie, barely able to contain himself, blurted out, "The rabbit's gone! Look, he's not in his cage!"

With a start, Chester looked at the empty cage sitting on the table by the window.

"Where do you suppose he is?" I asked.

"Quick," Chester commanded, "to the kitchen!"

"Where are you off to in such a rush?" Mrs. Monroe asked as we brushed by her legs. "You were just fed. I'm afraid no more food has miraculously reappeared in your dishes."

That's too bad, I thought, as we tumbled through the swinging kitchen door and skidded to a halt on the linoleum inside.

All was quiet. The refrigerator door was closed. A bowl of fruit sat undisturbed on the kitchen table. We listened attentively for breathing, or hopping, or whatever noises rabbits make when they've run away. There wasn't a sound.

"Gee, Pop, he's not here," Howie said.

Chester looked wildly about, his mind clicking away all the while. "We've got to warn the Monroes," he said at last. "Come on."

We dashed back into the living room. The boys had already gone upstairs, and my thoughts strayed to Toby, who was no doubt already settling into bed with his latest book and an array of snacks. If I didn't hurry to help him out, he'd be forced to eat them all by himself. I headed for the stairs. Chester grabbed me by the tail.

"Where do you think you're going?" he asked in a somewhat garbled voice.

"I'm just hearkening to the call of chocolate," I replied.

"Well, hearken to this before you go anywhere," he said. "We've got to alert the Monroes to what's going on. Now, you and Howie start whimpering. I'll jump up on Bunnicula's cage."

"Well, all right," I agreed somewhat reluctantly. "For Bunnicula's sake."

Mr. Monroe was turning out the lights. Mrs. Monroe stood at the bottom of the stairs ready to go up. A pile of clothes was in her arms. Howie and I ran to her side and whimpered pathetically.

"What's the matter?" she asked, her voice full

of concern. "Do you want some water?" She turned to her husband. "Robert, why don't you check their water dishes before coming up? I want to start folding this laundry."

I noticed that Chester had jumped up on the top of the cage, but as that part of the room was darkened already, no one paid any attention. Mrs. Monroe went up the stairs and Mr. Monroe into the kitchen. Chester jumped down.

When Mr. Monroe reentered, he stood looking down at us, shaking his head. "I don't know what your problem is, fellas," he said, "but you've got plenty of water." Once again, I started to whimper as Howie tugged at Mr. Monroe's pants leg. Chester, meanwhile, began hopping around the living room floor, looking as if he was trying to make his way over a patch of hot tar. Mr. Monroe just smiled at him. "Well, Chester, it looks as if you're still full of energy. Too bad we can't let you out. Good night."

He patted each of us and went to bed.

"Gee, Pop, are you okay?" Howie asked. "Can I help?"

"You can help by not being so dumb," Chester muttered, a look of disgust on his face. "I was trying to be a rabbit."

Howie became confused. "Why would you want to be a rabbit?" he asked. "Aren't you happy being a cat?"

I moved toward the stairs, the lure of crinkling cellophane (covering, I hoped, chocolate cupcakes) too strong to resist. Chester called after me.

"Harold, take the kid with you, will you? I've got to plan my strategy."

"I want to stay with you, Pop," Howie said.

Chester groaned.

"What strategy?" I asked.

"We've got to find that rabbit and return him to his cage before it's too late."

"Too late for what?" I asked. "I'm concerned about Bunnicula, too, but—"

"It's not the rabbit I'm worried about," he said. "It's *us,* you fool. I shudder to think what could happen in one little night with that bunny on the loose."

"Well," I replied, "I'll let you worry about

that. I've got bigger worries on my stomach—er, mind—right now."

I went up the stairs. I could hear Chester mumbling about rabbits and vegetables and vampires, and I knew his would be a restless night. But, I reassured myself, he would have Howie at his side to get him through. And what a comfort that would be.

After all, just as I turned the corner of the landing, didn't I hear Howie remark, "Well, Pop, you know what they always say?"

"No, son," Chester answered, "what do they always say?"

"Hare today, gone tomorrow."

TWO

Some Thoughts on Vegetables, or A Dead Beet in the Neighborhood

I WAS RUDELY awakened the next morning by Pete's crashlanding just inches from where I lay on Toby's bed.

"Wake up, wake up, you sleepy-creep!" Pete cried as he yanked his brother's pillow out from under his head and began badgering him with it. I was sorely tempted to pick Pete up by the tail-end of his pajamas and deposit him through the nearest open window, but decided this would not be particularly well-advised. Besides, I had morning mouth, and the thought of getting cotton all over my tongue gave me goose bumps. Yuck!

Toby, meanwhile, was screaming bloody murder.

"Help! Get out of here, Pete! What's the matter with you, anyway? Mom!" As he began kicking furiously at his attacker, I did the only sensible thing left open to me. I jumped off the bed and headed straight for the door.

As I left, I noticed Pete pull the sheet across the bottom half of his face and say, "Today eez the beeg day! Heh-heh-heh!"

That's a funny thing to say, I thought.

Some Thoughts on Vegetables

Pete's momentary stillness gave Toby an advantage. He knocked Pete's legs out from under him and went running out the door to the bathroom. I started down the stairs, narrowly missing being hit by the basketball that flew out of the bedroom and hit the closing bathroom door with a thud. It bounced back across the hall floor, causing the lighting fixture on the ceiling below to quake.

Boy, I thought, it'll be nice to get downstairs to some peace and quiet.

Mrs. Monroe stood at the bottom of the stairs. I whimpered good morning.

"Toby! Pete!" she greeted me in return. "Stop all that noise this minute! Peter, let your brother get dressed. Come down here and eat your breakfast. It's getting cold!"

As I sauntered across the living room, Mr. Monroe rushed into the house, letting the front door slam behind him. "You won't believe it," he said, "but the garage door's been open all night!"

"Oh, no!" Mrs. Monroe said. "Was anything taken? We're lucky no one broke into the house."

Pete charged down the stairs, skipping every other step. "What about the—" he started to say.

His father waved his hands in the air. "Everything's right where it belongs. Nothing's missing. We were lucky this time. But we'll have to be more careful in the future."

A delectable aroma reached my nostrils. I thought back to the yummy chocolate-chip cookies Toby had shared with me the night before and decided a slice or two of the nice crisp bacon presently burning on the kitchen stove would be a perfect follow-up treat this morning.

"Oh, no!" Mrs. Monroe cried. "The bacon!"

"Mom!" Toby called from upstairs. "The toilet's stuck. I think it's going to run over."

Mr. and Mrs. Monroe looked at each other and shook their heads.

"You to the bacon," Mr. Monroe said, "I to the toilet."

And I to the food dish, I thought.

Chester and Howie were already eating when I entered the kitchen with Mrs. Monroe.

"Good morning," I said cheerfully.

"Good morning, Uncle Harold," Howie yipped.

Chester, seemingly lost in thought—or at least in cat food—said not a word.

I was starved, but hesitated before digging in, hoping a little crumbled-up bacon might find its way to my dish. My hopes were not in vain.

"Great!" Mrs. Monroe said, whisking the sizzling frying pan off the stove. "Cold eggs and burned bacon. Well, this day is off to a terrific start. Here, fellas, it's all yours."

This day *is* off to a terrific start, I thought, as the bacon bits landed on my dish. Chester, who had still not said "good morning," didn't seem to share my attitude.

"What's the matter with you today?" I asked.

"Pop's had a rough night," I was informed by Howie.

"Oh," I said. "What happened, Chester?"

"Nothing happened," Chester's junior interpreter responded. "He just couldn't sleep, worrying."

"Oh, come on," I replied. "What's to worry

about? So Bunnicula got out. He'll come back. Everybody's in such a hurry around here this morning, maybe they're going out to look for him. Anyway, he'll be all right."

"It's not Bunnicula that Pop's worried about."

I turned to Chester. "Chester, have you lost your facility for speech?" I asked.

"Vegetables," Chester mumbled.

"What?"

"Vegetables," Howie echoed.

"Yes, thank you, Howie. I heard Chester. I just don't understand what he means."

"Follow me," Chester said, turning and walking out the kitchen door. His canine shadow trailed behind him.

"But . . . " I said, turning to my still-occupied food dish, " . . . but what about my breakfast?"

Turning over his shoulder, Chester replied, "This is important." And he vanished beyond the swinging door.

"Important," Howie repeated as he too disappeared from sight.

Hurriedly, I wolfed down the rest of my morning repast and, in a matter of seconds, was in the living room. Chester was perched on the arm of his favorite chair. Howie sat attentively at his feet.

Toby and Mr. Monroe came down the stairs to join the rest of the family in the kitchen. In his arms, Toby was clutching an overflowing shopping bag.

"I'm ready to go," he cried as he bounded through the kitchen door.

"Not until you've eaten," I heard his father say as he followed. "Then we'll be on our way."

Chester watched the swinging kitchen door slowly close, then turned to us.

"Has it ever occurred to you what happens to those vegetables?" he remarked.

"What vegetables?" I asked.

Chester looked deeply into my eyes. "The vegetables that Bunnicula attacks. The vegetables he drains of their life's juices. The vegetables, in short, he vampirizes!"

"Oh, *those* vegetables," I said.

"Those vegetables exactly. You see, Harold, I've given a great deal of thought to those vegetables during the night, and I have concluded . . . "

Howie, who had strayed from the conversation momentarily to attack a throw rug someone had been thoughtless enough to leave lying around on the floor, of all places, suddenly looked up.

"Pop's got this . . . um, what'd you call it again, Pop?"

"Theory," Chester said.

"Oh, yeah. He's got this theory, see, that—"

"Howie, dear boy," Chester interjected, "why don't you let me tell it, hmm?"

"Oh, sure, Pop, whatever you say," replied the dachshund agreeably. He returned to chewing the corner of the rug.

Chester went on. "I have this theory, Harold, that these vegetables, once attacked, are not as harmless as one might think."

"I never thought of vegetables as harmless," I said. "Especially spinach."

"What do we know from the literature of vampirism?" he continued. Seeing that I knew nothing from the literature of vampirism, he persevered. "We know that once attacked, the vampire's victims become their master's slaves. In fact, they are transformed into zombie-vampires, the living dead, doomed to go out into the night seeking fresh bodies to satisfy their bloody cravings."

"Chester," I said softly, "is this necessary right after breakfast?"

"It can't wait," he snapped. "We have to act fast."

"To do what?" I asked. "Surely you're not saying that these vegetables . . ."

"Do they just lie there, useless, finished, dried up?" Chester interrupted. "Or does Bunnicula, like the vampires of old, have a further purpose for them? Are they his minions acting on his orders to turn the world into creatures like himself? When night falls, are they out there waiting to lure innocent victims into taking a bite? Just one bite and . . . BAM! You're a goner! Think of it, Harold, if Bunnicula got out last night, this entire neighborhood could be filled with killer parsnips, blood-thirsty string beans, homicidal heads of lettuce—"

"Don't forget the minions," I said.

"What?"

"The minions who are acting on his orders. Are minions like onions, Chester?"

"A minion isn't a vegetable, you dolt. A minion is a follower, a servant."

"Oh."

I reflected for a moment on Chester's new theory. That's when I noticed Howie's whimpering. The poor fellow was cowering under the coffee table.

"What's the matter, Howie?" I asked.

"I'm afraid," he answered. "What if those killer parsnips sneak up on me while I'm sleeping and sink their fangs into my neck?"

I turned to Chester. "You see where your stories are getting us? Poor Howie's scared out of his wits."

"And rightly so, if my thinking is correct."

"But it isn't correct, Chester," I replied. "It's nonsense."

"We shall see, we shall see," Chester said, pulling at the hair between his toes. "But if the people in this town start acting strangely, it could be because Bunnicula and his vegetables have succeeded in. . . . Sshh! Say no more."

Chester bathed himself with sudden vigor as the entire Monroe family, laden with bundles, entered the living room. It looked as if they were headed for an outing of some kind. Well, why not? I thought. It's a beautiful day for a little romp in the great out-of-doors; I was all set to join them when Chester nudged me.

"Come on," he said, "we've got some checking up to do."

"But . . ."

"Goodbye, Chester. Goodbye, Harold," Mrs. Monroe said from where she stood by the front door. "Try to keep Howie and each other out of trouble while we're gone. If you want to go out, you can use the pet door. There's water in your dish and—"

"Dear," Mr. Monroe said, touching his wife gently on the arm, "the boys will be fine. Besides, we won't be gone long. We'll be back this afternoon."

"Yeah," Pete said. "Anyway, how do they

know what you're saying? They're just dumb animals."

Dumb animals! I thought. Hmmph! Pete had never been above talking to us before. I wondered if he was going through a stage. These days, it seemed as if Pete went through stages faster than socks.

Toby kicked his brother in the shins. "They are *not* dumb animals," he cried. I made a mental note to give Toby's face the reward of a thorough licking later. "They're smarter than you are."

"Don't make me laugh." Pete snorted.

"They are too."

"Are not."

"Are too."

"Are not."

"Boys!" Mrs. Monroe cried. "Please. Let's go."

Still bickering, Pete and Toby were led out the front door by their parents.

"Goodbye, fellas," Mr. Monroe called out over his shoulder as the front door clicked shut.

"Do you think we're smarter than Pete?" I asked Chester.

"*I* think we are, Uncle Harold," said Howie. "Why, just last week, Toby threw a stick in the backyard and Pete didn't even know enough to chase it and bring it back in his teeth. Even I know that."

Chester gazed at Howie through half-closed lids. "Well, there's your answer, Harold," he said. "Now, come on, we've got to move."

"Where are we going?" I asked as I followed Chester through the kitchen door.

"Outside," he answered. "We've got to find that rabbit and see what damage he's already done."

One after the other, we pushed through the pet door and onto the back porch.

"Ah!" I said, inhaling deeply. "What a day! Howie, I'll race you to that tree in the corner of the yard. Whoever falls asleep fastest wins."

"But how will we know?" Howie asked.

Chester cleared his throat. "Before you two tumble off into dreamland, remember what we came out here for. Wait a minute, what's that?"

Chester bounded down the stairs and headed in the direction of the garden. Howie and I followed closely behind. We stopped about ten feet from the garden's edge.

"There!" Chester exclaimed. "Do you see what I see?"

Squinting, I made out a round white object lying several feet away.

"What's so unusual about a rock?" I asked.

Chester's body hugged the ground as he slunk through the grass. Howie, whose body hugs the ground even when he doesn't slink, waddled behind. Chester came upon the object and batted at it tentatively.

As I drew closer, he pulled himself up to his full height and proclaimed dramatically, "A beet. A . . . drained . . . white . . . beet!"

"Oh, great," Howie said. "Before you know it, the whole neighborhood'll be full of dead beets."

Chester announced, "Bunnicula has been here!"

"Get it, Uncle Harold? Get it, Pop?" Howie's tail was wagging furiously. " 'Dead beets.' Get it, huh, get it?"

"Yes, Howie, very amusing," Chester said. "However, you seem to be missing the point. Bun-

nicula has been here. And he's left a vampire beet in his wake."

"Are you sure it's not a minion onion?" I asked cynically.

Howie began to shake again. "Does that mean . . . could it be . . . will it . . . oh, how am I going to sleep tonight?"

"Harold!" Chester snapped. "Grab that beet and run to the front of the house. We've got to warn the Monroes before they leave. Hurry!"

Being a born follower, and hoping to get this nonsense over with so I could get on to more important things, like sleep, I did as Chester bade me. As I rounded the corner of the house, Mr. Monroe was pulling the station wagon out of the driveway.

"Get their attention!" Chester cried. "Do something!"

"I can't, my mouth's full," I tried to say, but it came out sounding like, "Uk kn, mummumm-phoo."

"Howie!"

Howie reared back his head and let out a fearsome howl. "Aaah-ooooooooo!"

Chester's hair went up. "It really gives me the creeps when he does that," he said. But we saw the Monroes turn and look back through the car windows at us, so it must have done the trick.

They waved. "Goodbye, boys," they cried.

Mr. Monroe called out, "That's a good boy, Harold, you play with that old tennis ball. See you later!"

"Goodbye!"

"Goodbye!"

"Goodbye!"

"Ooo-oy!" I called out around the sides of the beet, which I quickly spat out. "Now what?" I asked. My mouth felt funny.

Howie and I regarded Chester, who seemed lost in thought.

After a moment, he turned to us.

"All right," he declared, his eyes getting that glaze I know means trouble ahead, "it's up to us. It's a big job that has to be done, but no job is too big for us, right, men?"

"Well . . . " I said.

"Right on, Pop!" shouted Howie gleefully.

"Let's go. Let's do it. Let's . . . by the way, what is it we're going to do?"

"You'll see," Chester replied. "Wait here." And he disappeared around the corner of the house.

[THREE]

Destiny Calls!

MOMENTS LATER, Chester reappeared from behind the house carrying a small box in his mouth. He trotted toward us and deposited the box at our feet.

Howie poked at it with his nose. "What's this?" he asked.

"Well, as you undoubtedly know," Chester explained, "in order to destroy a vampire, you have to drive a stake through its heart."

I groaned. "Not again! Don't you remember the last time you tried that?"

Chester immediately began bathing his tail, which is a cat's way of covering his humiliation.

"What happened?" asked Howie.

"Well," I said, "it seems Chester decided to drive a stake through Bunnicula's heart—"

"Oh, no!" Howie cried. "How could he?"

"That's a good question. With the kind of 'stake' Chester selected for the job, it *was* a little difficult. You see, he thought—"

"All right, all right," Chester spat out. "I made a little mistake. Everybody's entitled to one mistake in the course of a lifetime. But don't worry, Harold, I know what type of stake to use now. I've got just the thing."

I glanced at the box lying in the grass. "Toothpicks?" I asked.

"What better way to spear vegetables through the heart?"

"Toothpicks?" I asked again.

Chester glared at me. "Yes, toothpicks!" he snapped. "What's wrong with toothpicks?"

"Oh, nothing," I replied with a shrug. "If you want to make little white party hors d'oeuvres out of Bunnicula's victims . . . "

"We're not making little white party anythings," he shot back. "We're destroying killer vegetables."

"You tell him, Pop," Howie put in. I gave him a look. "Sorry, Uncle Harold," he said.

"And we're going to find Bunnicula, bring him back home where he belongs and save the people in this town from his evil ways."

"Okay, okay," I said. I agreed to go along, not because I was convinced that the townspeople were really in danger, but because I was worried about poor Bunnicula, out there all alone in the world. If anyone needed saving, it was he.

"Can I carry the toothpicks, Pop?" Howie asked.

"Sure, kid," Chester said agreeably. "But first . . . "

He selected a toothpick from the box and, with a sudden lunge that made Howie and me jump, neatly speared the white beet lying at our feet.

We gazed for a moment at Chester's handiwork.

"Whew, I'll bet that hurt," Howie said, shaking his head.

"Looks like an hors d'oeuvre to me," I commented.

"Well, now that the critics have been heard from," Chester said, "perhaps we can move on." He lifted his head and, with an air of great importance, began to swagger down the street. "Howie," he called back over his shoulder, "the toothpicks."

"Right, Pop," Howie replied, picking up the box with his teeth. I fell into step behind them, and off we went.

We walked for blocks. Cautiously, we peered into every driveway, every front porch, every open garage door we passed. Nowhere did we see anything out of the ordinary. Indeed, all over town people seemed to be going about their lives as usual. When, at length, I suggested to Chester that we do the same, he drew up short and looked me straight in the eye.

"Nonsense!" he exclaimed. "This is not a day for the ordinary, Harold. We can't turn back now. Destiny calls."

"Harold!" a far-off voice called out suddenly. I jumped and looked in amazement at Chester.

"Did you hear that?" I gasped. Chester nodded.

"Chester!" the voice cried.

Chester's eyes nearly popped out of his head, as he looked wildly about him.

"Could it be . . .?" I asked. "Is . . . is destiny really calling?"

"I d-don't know," Chester stammered.

"Harold! Chester!" the voice called again. This time it seemed nearer.

I could feel my knees start to quiver. Howie ran over and took refuge between my legs. He looked out sheepishly.

It was then that I turned and saw the familiar figure jogging up the sidewalk.

"Chester," I said with a sigh of relief, "look who's coming."

"Oh, no," he groaned in recognition.

"Hello, Max," I said to the approaching bull-dog. I noticed that he was wearing the same white turtleneck sweater I'd last seen him in. Chester and I had met Max at Chateau Bow-Wow, the kennel where we'd been boarded when the Monroes went on vacation.

"Hello, chaps," he said jovially. "I've been calling you and calling you. How've you been? Out for a little exercise?"

"Something like that," I said.

"Want to jog?" he asked.

"Uh, no thanks. Do you live around here?"

"Just moved in a while ago," he replied. "My family used to live on the other side of town. That's our house over there." He nodded over his shoulder.

"How do you like it?"

"Well, it's bully except for . . . " and he mumbled something that sounded like "next door" and pawed at the ground.

"Well, Max, it's been great chewing the fat with you," Chester said abruptly, "but we're on an important mission. No time to waste."

"Oh, really, Chester? And what may I ask are you up to?"

"We're in search of white vegetables! Seen any?"

Max gave Chester a puzzled look, then shrugged. "Well, I don't know what you want with 'em, but yes, I have seen some, as a matter of fact. Darndest thing; got up this morning, went out to dig up a bone I'd buried in the garden last week, and what do you think I saw?"

Howie dropped his box of toothpicks. "The early bird getting the worm?" he asked.

"Heh, heh, heh," chuckled Max. "Clever little whippersnapper, isn't he? No, young fella, what I saw was—"

"White vegetables!" Chester finished the sentence for him.

"Right on the money there, Chester. There must have been . . . oh, three or four at least . . . lying about the garden."

"Are they still there?" Chester asked.

Max turned down the corners of his already turned-down mouth. "Guess so," he said. "I don't know where they'd've gone to."

"Right!" said Chester. "Let's go. That house over there, you say?"

"That's right," Max replied.

"You want to join us?" I asked.

"Uh, no thanks, Harold, ol' boy," Max replied. "I've had enough adventures for one day, if it's all the same to you." It was then that I noticed Max's face was covered with scratches.

"What happened to you?" I asked.

At first he didn't answer. Then, gazing off into the distance, he said softly, "Snowball."

"Huh?"

"Snowball," he repeated. Then, almost in a daze, he wandered off down the street, muttering to himself under his breath.

That was strange, I thought, as I trotted along to catch up with Howie and Chester. But then, Max always was a little peculiar. I wondered what he meant by "Snowball."

I rounded the corner of the big yellow house Max had indicated was his to find Chester and Howie making stabs at what looked like a large white rutabaga. Their toothpicks kept breaking.

"Boy, this one's tough," Howie said. I noticed two other white objects lying nearby with toothpicks already sticking out of them. With a great deal of effort, Chester finally succeeded in getting the rutabaga to accept its toothpickled fate.

"Whew," Chester said, wiping his brow. He looked around him at the rest of the garden. "Doesn't look as if there are any more to take care of here."

Howie scanned the garden as well. "No more here," he echoed. Then he attacked a hose lying nearby. Growling, he wrestled with it, ignoring the fact that the sprinkler at the other end was bouncing and splashing all over the garden.

"Try not to leave teethmarks," I advised.

"Come on, Howie, knock it off," Chester said. "We've got to keep moving. You can play later." He started off in the direction of the street when he came to a sudden halt.

"What if—" he said, shaking his head. "No, he couldn't have. Not in one night. Still . . . "

"What are you talking about?" I asked.

Howie let out a yelp as water spurted into his eye. He began barking furiously at the leaking hose.

"Nice work," I observed. "You've not only left teethmarks, you've expanded the sprinkler system. May I suggest we get out of here . . . fast?"

"Wait a minute," said Chester. Howie ran up to Chester's side, no doubt seeking his protection from the attacking garden hose. "I just had a thought. What if Bunnicula's met up with one of his own kind? You know how they multiply, Harold."

"Well, I don't really," I replied. "But if they're like everybody else these days, they probably use those little pocket calculators. I would, except my paws are too big. I hit all the numbers at once. So I have to do it the old way, and I never could get the hang of it. Let's see, four times six is eighteen. Or is it thirty-two? Or—"

Chester bopped me on the nose with his paw.

"Ouch!"

"Not that kind of multiplying, you twit."

"Oh."

"I'm talking about reproduction."

I was aghast. "Shh," I said, "not in front of the child."

"Oh, it's all right, Uncle Harold," said Howie, who'd overheard the whole conversation. "I know all about that stuff. And Pop is right, rabbits really do multiply like crazy."

"Right," Chester said. "Let's just hope we're not too late. Come on."

Wondering how it was that Howie knew so much more about reproduction than barbecues or garden hoses, I lumbered off behind Chester. I was so lost in thought that I didn't even hear him when he began yelling.

"It's him!" I made out at last. "It's Bunnicula! Harold, get over here." I ran to join Chester and Howie, who were huddled behind a bush. Chester was looking in the direction of the house next door. There on a porch railing perched a furry white animal. A shadow fell across it so I couldn't completely make it out, but it did look an awful lot like our missing rabbit.

"Grab him!" Chester commanded. "You're the only one who can do it, Harold. Get him in your teeth and carry him on home."

"Oh, Chester," I protested, "you know how I hate getting hair in my mouth. Besides, he looks so peaceful lying there like that. Couldn't we come back and get him later?"

"Later!? Later?!" Chester fairly shrieked. "Don't you understand anything, Harold? Later may be too late. Get him now!"

He pushed at my haunches, and I set off toward the porch.

"Get him, Uncle Harold!" Howie cried.

With a leap, I grabbed the sleeping rabbit in my mouth and took off down the street.

"That's it, Uncle Harold!" I heard Howie call out behind me. "Take the bunny and run!"

I'm sorry, Bunnicula, I thought, I really didn't want to do this. Hopefully, you'll sleep through the whole thing, and when we get you home, I'll tuck you into your little bed in your little cage and

you'll be nice and cozy and—

That's when I heard the woman scream.

"Help! Help!"

I looked over my shoulder. Howie and Chester were close behind. On the porch, where moments before the rabbit had been napping, stood a woman waving her arms in our direction.

"Help! Someone! Police! He's got my cat! My precious cat! My . . . my . . . Snowball!"

Snowball! My mind reeled as I thought of Max's scratched-up face.

As best I could, I looked down at the object I was carrying in my mouth. Its eyes turned upward to meet mine. There was a gleam in them, a gleam that spelled trouble with a capital S-N-O-W-B-A-L-L.

I gulped. Snowball hissed. The woman on the porch screamed.

"Help!"

You can say that again, lady, I thought. For both of us!

[FOUR]

An Unexpected Journey

OH, WHY couldn't you be a real snowball and melt? I thought as I raced down the street. The cat hanging from my jaws showed no signs of melting; rather, with his hair fluffed out in all directions, he seemed to be growing bigger with each passing second. Chester, I thought, I'm

going to get you for this one, I really am. *If* I live.
I looked around me, trying to figure out what to do
next.

Chester and Howie came up on my right.

"Toss him!" Chester cried out as he moved into
earshot.

"I'll take him, Uncle Harold," Howie barked
excitedly. "I'm not afraid of cats."

That's because you haven't lived long enough,
kid, I thought.

Behind me, Snowball's owner, swinging a
broom, was fast approaching. I looked to my right.
Wide open street. To my left. Wide open lawn.
No safe place to ditch the bristling cat.

But just then, I noticed a mailman coming up
the sidewalk in my direction. Behind him he pulled
a cart. As I ran past, I flung Snowball into the mail-
cart and hightailed it as fast as I could to the nearest parked car. Under I went. Chester and Howie
were already cowering behind one of the wheels.

We looked out to see envelopes and magazines
and packages flying helter-skelter out of the cart
and landing all over the sidewalk. Flashes of white

fur passed into view from time to time as Snowball tried frantically to escape. Not knowing what
else to do, the mailman stood by helplessly, his
eyes wide in amazement, his mouth hanging open.

Suddenly, all movement came to an abrupt halt.
Then, two white ears crept up over the edge of
the cart. The top of a head surfaced. Two dark
eyes came into view. Two dark eyes . . . staring
right into mine. My heart sank. My stomach sank.
Even my toenails sank. Doomed, I thought, I'm
doomed.

Just as Snowball was about to jump out and
seal my fate, his owner swept up from behind
and scooped him into her loving (and, fortunately
for me, strong) arms. As she carried him off toward home, he looked back over her shoulder
and shook a clenched paw in my direction.

Riveted to the spot, I watched the mailman
bend down and slowly pick up piece after piece of
scattered mail.

"Boy, did you see that stuff fly?" Howie whispered. "I guess that's what they call 'air mail,'
huh?"

"Nice work, Chester," I said after I'd caught my breath. My heart was still pounding like a jack-hammer.

"A small error of judgment," Chester replied calmly. "Everyone's entitled to one small error of judgment."

"Remind me to be comforted by that when Snowball uses my face as a scratching post," I said.

Chester regarded me coolly. "Tsk, tsk, tsk," he said, "a big dog like you afraid of a little kitty-cat? What kind of example are you setting for young Howie here?"

I was about to set an example for young Howie by sitting on Chester when he suddenly scurried to the other side of the car.

"Look!" Chester cried.

Howie and I joined him and gazed across the street. There, on the opposite sidewalk, we saw what looked like dozens of feet moving down the block.

"Where is everyone going?" Chester asked.

"I don't know," I replied. "What do you make of it?"

"I'm not sure. But there's something strange about the way those people are moving. Almost as if they were all going to the same place. Look, they're crossing the road. Why?"

"To get to the other side?" Howie suggested.

Chester didn't respond. He was too busy watching the people move off down the street.

"What if . . . what if . . . " he said suddenly. "What if they've already fallen victim to Bunnicula and his zombie vegetables? Let's follow them."

"Ernie," a voice called out from behind us just as we were about to move out from under the car, "did you get those white vegetables that were out in the garden this morning?"

Our ears perked up. We dashed to the other side and looked out from behind a wheel. A man was dumping lawn clippings into a big plastic garbage pail by the sidewalk. His wife was calling to him from the front porch of their house.

"I sure did," the man named Ernie replied to the woman's question. "Wasn't that the weirdest thing? I've never seen white vegetables before. Didn't know what to think. Anyway, I put them in the pail with the weeds."

"We've got to find them," Chester whispered urgently.

"But Chester, I thought you wanted to follow that crowd of people."

"First things first," he replied.

The man picked up the full garbage pail and carried it to a pick-up truck parked in the drive-way. I noticed that the truck contained several other pails filled with clippings.

"I'm going to take this stuff down to the dump myself," the man proclaimed. "No sense waiting for the sanitation men when there's so much of it."

"Good idea," his wife agreed. "Wait a minute. I'll give you the garbage from the party last night. We may as well get rid of that at the same time." She went inside the house as the man hoisted the garbage pail over the side of the truck.

"How are we going to find those vegetables now?" I asked. "They're somewhere inside one of those pails."

"Obviously we're going to have to look for them."

"But how?" I protested. "When? The man's leaving for the dump any minute."

"And guess who's going with him?"

"Oh, now, wait a minute . . . "

"Are we going for a ride, Pop?" Howie piped up.

"That's the general idea."

"Oh, boy!"

"Now, hold on there, Chester," I said. "I didn't bargain for a sightseeing tour of the town dump in today's activities. Besides, you know I get carsick. I'll . . . I'll stay here and . . . and look for Bunnicula."

Chester wasn't having any of my arguments. "It'll be faster with all three of us looking," he said. "Besides, the trip to the dump can't take all that long. We'll be there and back before you know it."

The man was inside the truck starting the engine as his wife emptied the extra garbage over the side.

"See you soon, dear," she said as he started to

pull out of the driveway. She went back into the house, and Chester said, "Now's our chance. Let's go."

Chester and I jumped up and over the edge of the truck in one gazelle-like movement. But Howie, who lacks the agility—not to mention the legs—of a gazelle, succeeded only in falling over backward onto the gravel. Frantically, he scampered back and forth by the side of the truck, yipping his head off.

"Sshhh! Harold, get him!" Chester advised.

I leaned over the side and scooped poor Howie up by the scuff of his neck just as the truck turned into the street. With a flip, he landed in the garbage pail next to me.

"This has been a great day for my mouth," I commented, trying to spit out the dog and cat hairs that coated my tongue. "Do you suppose we could stop for a lemonade?"

Chester gave me a look.

"Let's start digging," he said.

Just then, Howie's head popped up out of the

garbage pail. Strands of spaghetti cascaded over his forehead and ears, as tomato sauce ran down the sides of his nose.

"Boy," he said, licking his chops and catching the rivulets of sauce with his tongue, "that must have been some party they had last night."

The Dog in
the Green Toupée

C'MON, HOWIE," Chester said, "quit clowning around. We've got serious business to take care of."

"Who's clowning?" asked Howie, licking his lips. He ducked back down into the garbage pail, his voice calling out from its depths. "There's some great stuff in here. Corncobs. Melon rinds. Apple strudel. Whipped cream. Oh, and here's a nice, big, juicy—"

And then all I could hear was a loud crunch.

Chester sighed heavily. "Harold," he muttered, "could you do something about Howie, please? I believe I'm about to have heart palpitations."

I looked at my friend Chester and shook my head. "No one ever said it was easy being a father," I commented.

"Very funny," he replied. "Now, would you please ask the kid to knock it off?"

I must admit my mouth was watering for a little of that apple strudel, but I decided it would have to wait. After all, my digestive tract would know no peace with Chester champing at the bit the way he was. I knocked on the side of the pail and entreated Howie to remove himself.

Reluctantly, he agreed.

"Can you help me get out of here?" he asked. "I think my foot's stuck in a ketchup bottle or something."

"Here," I said, jumping up against the side of the pail. "I'll pull you out. Just grab my neck."

Chester backed away. "Be careful you don't pull the whole thing . . . " he was saying when my foot slipped on a banana skin Howie must have thrown out earlier.

"Whoops!" I cried. I fell back as Howie and the garbage pail came tumbling down. Howie flew past my head. The pail's contents spilled all over the floor.

And Chester.

And me.

Nervously, I shot a glance to the front of the truck to see if the driver had heard the crash, but he must have been playing his radio really loudly, because he didn't even turn around.

When I turned back, Chester was staring at me. A watermelon rind sat on the top of his head like an oversized beret. His face was plastered with seeds.

"Gee, it looks like you've grown some freckles since I saw you last," I joked.

Chester wasn't in a laughing mood. He shook off the remains of the watermelon and suggested I do the same with the tea bags and coffee grounds that adorned my head.

Howie, meanwhile, was contentedly chewing on a steak bone that had landed at his side.

"Any more where that came from?" I asked eagerly.

Howie didn't reply; he was too busy slurping over his find.

"Later, Harold, later," Chester muttered. "Right now, we've got to see if we can find those vegetables." He gazed into the overturned pail. "Wait a minute," he cried suddenly. "There, next to those cans, doesn't that look like a . . . I'm going in to take a look around. Harold, start checking the other pails." And he disappeared from sight.

With Chester out of the way, I was all set to root through the garbage that was strewn about to see if I could find something good to eat, when the truck suddenly swerved to the right and my stomach lurched to the left. I groaned. There's nothing like a sudden case of carsickness, I thought, to knock the appetite right out of you.

"Boy, this bone is great," Howie remarked just then. "It could use a little seasoning though. Would you pass that jar of peanut butter, Uncle Harold?"

As the truck veered around a bend in the road, I moaned and batted the peanut-butter jar toward Howie. Nauseated, I made my way toward a still-standing garbage pail and began snooping around. What do dead vegetables smell like? I wondered as I poked my nose under the lid. The odor of freshly cut grass greeted my nostrils.

Oh, no! I thought, a sudden rash of panic running through me. My hay fever! I could feel that familiar tingle in the end of my nose.

"Aah . . . ah . . . ah-choo!"

The lid of the garbage pail flipped over as hundreds of blades of grass sailed into the air. After riding the currents for a brief, liberating fling, they tumbled down, one after the other, to nestle into their new home on the top of my head, sticking to the wet spot the coffee grounds had so recently made ready for them.

Howie looked up from his repast and chuckled at what he saw. "Gee, Uncle Harold," he said, "you'd make a great title for a spy novel: *The Dog in the Green Toupée.*"

"Ha . . . ah . . . ha . . . ah . . . choo!" I replied.

Chester emerged from the pail just then, dragging in his teeth a stalk of celery.

"Boy," I said, trying to shake off the stubbornly clinging grass, "you smell terrible. What'd you get into in there, anyway?"

"You don't smell like a rose yourself," he said, dropping the celery. "Anyway, it doesn't matter what else is in there, the important thing is that I've found the white vegetables. Or some of them, at least. I'll bring out the rest and then we can get to work."

Chester withdrew once again into the inner recesses of the pail only to return several times with various specimens of vegetable specters. He

laid them out neatly on the floor of the truck, his appraising eye passing over each in turn.

"How do you know that celery's one of the culprits?" I asked. "After all, celery is white to begin with."

"Sometimes," Chester said. "And sometimes, it's green. Anyway, we can't be too careful. We wouldn't want to leave a killer celery stalk on the loose, would we?"

"Well, I hope you're right," I muttered. "If not, we may be getting a phone call from the Society for the Prevention of Cruelty to Vegetables."

"Thank goodness we found them in time," Chester went on with a sigh. "Howie, bring the toothpicks over here."

Howie glanced up from his bone, a look of bewilderment on his face. "Toothpicks?" he asked.

"Yes."

Howie, his lips covered with peanut butter, smiled weakly. "I think I forgot them, Pop. I must have left them back at the garden behind Max's house. Gee, I'm sorry. I . . . uh . . . "

The tip of Chester's tail tapped the floor nervously.

"Great," he said, "that's just great. Now what're we going to do?"

"Well," I replied, "before your heart palpitations start up again, I think I have a solution. Inside that pail over there," I went on, indicating the one that had exploded its contents all over my head, "there are a lot of twigs. They're a little big for the job, but I don't see any reason we couldn't use them instead of toothpicks."

Chester considered my suggestion and, after a moment's reflection, nodded solemnly. "I like it," he said. "It's . . . it's natural, organic, back-to-the-earth. Thoreau would have been proud of you."

Well, I wasn't sure what Thoreau had to do with it (in fact, I wasn't sure who Thoreau was, though I had a sneaking suspicion he'd once pitched for the Yankees), but I decided to accept Chester's response with modest appreciation. After all, a compliment from Chester is something like a shooting star: rare, and if you blink, there's a good chance you'll miss it.

We picked out several likely candidates for stakehood from among the twigs and, with great ceremony, drove them through the hearts of the vampirical veggies.

We were admiring our work when all at once we heard a loud BANG!

"They're shooting!" Howie cried. He covered his ears with his paws. "Don't let them get me, Uncle Harold," he whimpered. "I'll give them back their steak bone. I didn't mean to take it, honest I didn't. Just don't let them shoot me. I'm too young to die. I'm too nice to die. I'm too *me* to die."

"Will you cut that out?" Chester snapped. "Nobody's shooting."

"How can you be sure?" I asked. "Maybe there's a law against stabbing vegetables with twigs in the back of a moving pick-up truck." I lowered myself to the floor, getting out of the line of fire.

I became aware then that our ride had become very bumpy. And that we were slowing down. The truck pulled off the road and rolled unevenly to a complete stop.

Before we could figure out what was going on, the driver jumped out and walked to the rear end of the truck. "Great," I heard him mumble, "a flat! Just what I needed!"

He lowered the tailgate. "Well," he went on, "I'll just get the spare and . . . well, well, well, what have we here?"

I looked up to see him staring straight at me. I tried to smile.

"Where did *you* come from?" he asked, startled.

Don't ask me, I thought, *they're* the experts on reproduction.

He stood there scratching his head. "Boy, what a mess you've made. Come on, get out of there. Let's go." He swatted at us, indicating in his unsubtle way that the ride was over.

For my part, it didn't take much persuading. I was relieved our little adventure had come to an end. Between the garbage and the hayfever and the carsickness, I was delighted to say goodbye to the truck and feel solid ground underfoot once again.

As the three of us walked along the highway toward town, I said to Chester, "I'll be glad to get home."

"So will we all," Chester said wearily. "So will we all. But first . . . "

"Yeah, yeah, I know," I said. "Destiny calls."

"Exactly."

"Harold! Chester!" a distant voice cried out.

We stopped in our tracks.

"Chester," I said, shaking slightly. "Did you hear . . . "

"Yes, I—"

"Harold!" the voice called again. "Chester!"

Chester's eyes went wild. "It isn't Max this time," he said. "It must be . . . "

Then we heard the sound of someone laughing.

We turned and saw Howie standing several feet behind us, a grin plastered on his face from ear to ear.

"Boy, Pop. Boy, Uncle Harold. You really fell for it. Heh, heh, heh."

Chester and I looked at each other.

"Harold, can't you do a better job of keeping

the kid in line?" Chester asked me as we resumed walking.

"I don't know, Chester," I replied, "he's *your* son."

And Howie kept chuckling all the way into town.

The Transformation
of Toby and Pete

BY THE TIME we reached the sign that said,
"Welcome to Centerville . . . The Place
That People Who Live Here Call Home," I was

feeling better. There's something about a leisurely walk in the country, regardless of the circumstances, that invigorates the soul and reminds one that the simple pleasures are the best. After all, what could be more gratifying than a stroll down a country lane with your two best friends, even when the country lane is in reality a four-lane super highway complete with speeding cars and bleating horns, and one of your two best friends is getting a migraine trying to read the writing on the spinning hubcaps, while the other is ranting and raving about killer vegetables, and all three of you reek of eau de garbage? One must learn to overlook such minor drawbacks and take one's enjoyment where one can. Which is exactly what I was doing late that Saturday morning when Chester suddenly went into his stalking position.

He scampered behind a rock, wiggled his rear end, and flattened his head so that no one on the other side could see him.

"What's up?" I asked innocently, sauntering up to his side. Howie joined us a second or two later. "Let me guess. You've just seen a suspicious-

looking string bean hanging out in the cabbage
patch."

"And you're waiting to see if the rice squad
shows up, " Howie chimed in.

Chester was not amused.

"Ssh," he admonished us.

"But what . . . "

"Over there," Chester said, "across the road.
You want suspicious-looking, Harold, I'll give
you suspicious-looking. What's wrong with that
picture?"

My gaze drifted to the house across the road.
I saw that in its front yard was gathered a small
group of kids. One of them was standing apart
from the others. Though I looked them over care-
fully, I was unable to discern anything peculiar
going on.

When I said nothing, Chester went on. "Their
clothes, Harold," he said. "Look at what they're
wearing. I ask you—is that normal?"

I saw then that two of the kids were wearing
long black capes—the one standing alone and another who seemed to be pushing several others

forward. When I looked more closely, I was in for an even greater surprise.

"That's Toby and Pete!" I cried.

"Not so loud," Chester replied. "I know that's Toby and Pete. But I don't want them to hear us."

"Why don't you want them to hear us?" I asked.

"Yeah, Pop, why don't you want them—"

"I have my reasons," Chester said. "Come on, we've got to get closer and listen in. Follow me."

I must admit it did seem a little strange for Toby and Pete to be wearing capes, but having lived in a house with two normal, active boys for many years, I had come to expect the unexpected. Heck, I'd lived with Chester for many years. And if that hadn't taught me to expect the unexpected, nothing ever would.

Stealthily, we crept along the edge of the road, and when we saw that no cars were coming, hurried across to find a good hiding place behind a rhododendron bush.

I could see clearly then that it was Pete who was standing off to one side and Toby who was pushing the others toward him. What we over-heard was curious. Very curious indeed.

"Here they are, Master," Toby said, shoving several of the boys and girls forward. "I caught them snooping around."

Pete said, "You did, eh? Good work. Now, what shall we do with them, hmm?"

One of the kids in the group spoke up angrily. "We didn't mean anything, honest. We just wanted to know what was going on. We didn't think—"

"You didn't think is right," Pete shot back, swirling his cape over his arm. "You don't know who I am, do you? Well, you'll find out. You'll find out. Take them away!"

Toby started to push the kids toward the back of the house as they cried, "No, no, no!"

"What do you think is going on?" I whispered to Chester. "It's not like Peter and Toby to be so rough."

"Maybe they're just playing," Howie suggested.

"I don't think so," Chester replied softly. "There's something too serious in their manner."

We noticed then that Pete was telling Toby to wait a moment. "Hello, what's this?" Chester asked as his ears lifted.

Pete was pointing at one of the girls in the group. "Don't take that one," he instructed Toby. "Leave her with me."

"Me?" the girl cried out in alarm. "No, please, I beg you."

Toby pushed the girl forward and she fell on her knees. He left with the other kids, disappearing around the corner of the house. Pete stared at the girl for a long, tense moment.

"What is your name?" he asked at last.

"Hilda," the girl replied, her voice shaking slightly.

"Hilda," Pete repeated. "What a charming name. You are new to our little town, are you not?"

"Yes, I just moved here."

"I thought I'd never seen you before. Get up. Come closer."

Slowly, the girl stood. But she didn't move any nearer to Pete. She seemed scared of him.

"Come, come," Pete said, "there's nothing to be afraid of."

That's what I was thinking, I thought. That's just old Pete. Why would anybody be afraid of him? He's a creep sometimes, it's true. I remembered the time he painted a white stripe down Chester's back because he wanted a pet skunk. But still . . .

"I'm not afraid," the girl said. "It's just—"

"Just what?" Pete tilted his head to one side.

"I've heard about you. I've heard . . . things . . . "

Pete chuckled. "What sort of things?" he asked.

"About what goes on here."

Slowly, Pete moved toward the girl. She didn't move. When he was just inches away from her, he said, "How lovely your neck is."

Well, I was surprised at that one, I can tell you. As far as I knew, Pete didn't like girls. He'd certainly never noticed their necks before. Or said mushy things like that.

"So white," he went on, "so pure, so . . . "

He didn't finish. Instead, much to my amazement, he lunged for her neck and appeared to be

[82]

biting it. Chester, Howie and I gasped. The girl fell to the ground. And Pete, wiping his mouth with his arm, laughed like a maniac.

"I can't believe it," Chester muttered. "It's happened. It's really happened."

"What's happened, Pop?"

"Yeah, what?" I asked. "Pete finally likes girls?"

"No, you dimwit. He . . . shh . . . listen!"

Toby came around from back of the house.

"Did you take care of the others?" Pete asked him.

"Yes, Master, just as you told me to."

Just then, another kid came running up the street and into the yard. He too was wearing a black cape.

"Come on, let's go," he called out. "It's time. The others are waiting."

Pete and Toby jumped up and down, laughing. "It's our time at last," Toby cried out gleefully. "Time for the vampires!"

"On to Castle Bunnicula!" Peter shouted, and they all broke out in demonic giggles.

"We've got to stop them!" Chester said, his voice shaking with excitement. "It's happened, don't you see? Bunnicula and his zombie vegetables have finally gotten to real human beings. I'm not surprised that it's our own Toby and Pete who are the ringleaders. I always knew they were too susceptible. All that television had to take its toll one day. And now . . . and now . . . oh, I can't believe it. Vampires! Come on, you two, we've got to get there and warn the others."

"Get where?" I asked.

"Where they've rounded everybody up."

"Gee," I said, "remember that crowd of people we saw earlier? Do you suppose—"

"Of course!" Chester replied, cutting me off. "They've got them all in their power. Hurry, it's up to us to save what's left of Centerville."

Once again that day, I found myself racing down the street. I must admit that this time I was really worried. A drastic change had come over Toby and Pete. Were they gone forever? I thought, as I hurried behind Chester. No more chocolate snacks at twilight, no more games of catch in the backyard, no more tummy rubs?

"Hey, Harold! Chester! Come here, Howie!" I looked back and saw Toby calling us. "Come on, you guys! Where're you going?"

I hesitated for a moment. Maybe it was all a dream. Maybe if I went to them, they'd be just ol' Toby and ol' Pete and everything would be the same.

I whimpered, longing for things to go back to the way they were.

"Don't turn back, Harold," Chester cried out. "That's just what they want you to do. Don't be a fool! Keep moving! They'll turn you into a vampire . . . or a werewolf . . . or . . ."

"Ahh-oooooooooo!" Howie yowled, throwing back his head.

Chester shuddered. "Of course, in some cases, we may already be too late," he said.

"Sorry, Pop," Howie called out. "I just had to get that off my chest."

Everything became a blur as we ran faster and faster. Where we were headed I didn't know. But what we were running from was clear.

"Hey, you guys, come here!" Toby called.

"Here, Harold! Here, Chester! Here, Howie!" Pete chimed in.

Chester is right, I thought. Bunnicula really is a vampire. He really does have minion onions. And now he's got Toby and Pete, too. Who knows who else in our humble little town has fallen into his clutches? We may be too late to save them all, but we'll save whomever we can, however we can.

Watch out, Centerville, here we come!

SEVEN

Curse of the Vampires

ON AND ON WE RAN, racing breathlessly past the post office, the Acme Supermarket, the Starlight Lounge and Bowlarama. In the distance, I made out a throng of people moving toward an iron gate that stood ready to swallow them up into the yard of a long brick building.

Castle Bunnicula! I thought, though I must say that even then the building didn't look too much like a castle anything.

As we drew closer to the milling crowd, Chester cried out, "Mindless zombies! Hypnotized, lost, hopeless. We'll save them, Harold! We're almost there, I can feel it!"

I glanced back to see that Toby and Pete and their gang of fiendish hoodlums were still on our tails. Faster, faster I went, dodging honking cars and wobbly bicycles, whose riders called out words of encouragement and support like, "Hey, you stupid dog, watch where you're going!"

Howie's little legs scampered by as he shouted, "Aren't we having fun, Uncle Harold? This is better than eating shoes!"

Chester ran through the crowd and the iron gate. "This way!" he called back to us. "Follow me!"

Howie and I bounded through the gate to find ourselves in the midst of a swarm of people milling about, shouting, laughing, carrying on. What a festive air, I thought, for people doomed to a fate worse than death. I thought no further then as I spotted Chester at the far end of the crowd. He was jumping onto a large platform on which stood a youngster who didn't seem to notice his arrival. Instead, the kid waved his hands in the air and called out above the heads of the crowd, "Here we are! We're all ready!"

I glanced behind me and saw that he was shouting to Toby and Pete, who were leading the pack fast catching up with us.

"Hurry!" Chester called to us. "Faster! Faster!"

Through the crowd we raced madly, bumping into legs everywhere we went.

"Watch it!" someone cried.

"Who let those animals in here?" shouted another.

"Oops!!"

"Stop them! Catch them!"

"Mad dogs!"

I looked up to see people lunging toward me. A look of fierce determination glinted in several pairs of eyes. Possessed, I thought; out to get us to join their vampire ranks. I jerked out of the way of their advances, shepherding Howie safely through.

A fat man in a bright yellow shirt suddenly blocked our way.

"Here, doggie. Come on, little pup," he said menacingly.

"Be careful!" Chester warned. "Don't look him in the eye or it's all over!"

I darted through the man's legs. He fell forward, narrowly missing squashing Howie, who fortunately moved to the side just in time. I crashed into a little kid, transplanting the ice cream cone he was eating from his fist to his forehead.

"Mommy!" he screeched.

I jumped up onto the platform, knocking over the kid who'd been calling to Toby and Pete.

"What the—" he cried out in surprise as he picked himself up.

"Uncle Harold! Uncle Harold!" Howie called. I dashed back to the platform's edge to pick Howie up with my teeth.

"Now what?" I asked Chester, dropping Howie

on the platform next to me.

Chester looked around him. "This must be their headquarters," he confided quietly. Then, taking a big breath, he screamed, "Destroy! Demolish! Charge!"

I barked loudly as I dashed about, tumbling into chairs and tables, scattering a scatter rug, unearthing a plant, sending a cup and saucer flying. Howie tugged at the pants leg of the kid still standing on the platform.

"Cut it out!" the kid yelled, trying to shake Howie off. "What's with you, anyway?"

Chester jumped from one overturned object to another, emitting unearthly yowls as he went.

In short, we made quite a scene.

And it wasn't over yet. Just as I thought we'd done about as much damage as we could do, I heard a loud, creaking sound.

"Watch out!" someone in the crowd yelled.

"It's falling! Move out of the way!"

The kid jerked his pants leg out of Howie's mouth, and scrambled out of the way and over the edge of the platform.

"Move, Harold!" I heard Toby cry. "It's going to fall right on your—"

It was then that I glanced up and saw what looked like a wall falling right in my direction. Down it came . . . right toward me. I had enough time to notice a portrait hanging on the wall. And then, with a CRASH, the portrait was hanging on me!

Pretty flimsy construction, I thought, as I surveyed the scene and saw that the "wall" was nothing more than cloth stretched over some pieces of wood. No wonder it hadn't hurt when it had smashed over my head.

I didn't have time to observe much else as I heard Chester yelling, "Look, over there, it's Mrs. Monroe. She's holding a giant white carrot! Undoubtedly the leader of the vampire vegetables. I've got to destroy it!"

I watched as he raced through the crowd and leaped into the air just feet away from where Mrs. Monroe was standing. He smashed into the carrot she was holding in her hands. He must have jumped with a lot of force because the carrot

seemed to disintegrate before my eyes. It splat-
tered into the air, all over the ground and over
Chester, who at the moment was sliding off the
plate the stunned Mrs. Monroe still held in her
hands.

Just then, Howie tugged at my hair. "Uncle
Harold!" he said with great alarm in his voice.

"Yes? Ouch!"

"They're drowning Mr. Monroe! Look! He
must have resisted, and now they're drowning
him!"

I looked past the crowd, past Mrs. Monroe and
Chester, and saw that, sure enough, Mr. Monroe
was in the process of being drowned. There he
sat, on a little seat above a pool of water when
suddenly . . . the seat gave way and . . . *splash!*
. . . down he went!

"I'll save you!" I barked. I dashed off the platform and through the crowd and without thinking
of what I was doing (heroic type that I am)
jumped into the pool of water. Boy, was it cold!

Even my teeth were shivering as I grabbed Mr.
Monroe by his shirt collar and pulled him to the

side. For some reason, he was laughing. Hysterical, I thought, the poor man's gone over the edge. But, no, he seemed to be laughing at *me.*

"It's all right, Harold," I heard him say, "no one is trying to hurt me. It's a game, just a game."

Huh? Now I was really confused. What was going on here anyway?

I looked up to see other people laughing as well. Were they laughing at me? Mrs. Monroe came through the crowd as Mr. Monroe and I departed the pool. Someone handed Mr. Monroe a towel. I shook the water off as best I could, to the squeals of surprise of several bystanders. Mrs. Monroe didn't appear to be as amused as the other people.

"What in the world's come over them?" she asked.

Toby and Pete pushed their way through. Toby was carrying a bedraggled-looking Howie under his arm. Chester was suspended by the scruff of his neck from the hand of the irate Pete.

"They've ruined everything!" Pete cried.

Ruined? I thought. We saved the day!

Didn't we?

"Yeah, Mom," Toby whined. "Look what they did to our play!"

Play?

I turned my head and saw for the first time the sign hanging atop the platform.

"Curse of the Vampires!" it read. "A Play by Toby and Peter Monroe. 1:00 Today!"

I turned and glared at Chester. As best he could in his awkward position, he shrugged.

"Yeah," Pete went on, "I think they've gone crazy or something. We were up at Kyle's house, practicing our parts, when all of a sudden, the three of them jumped out from behind this bush and took off down the street."

"We called to them and everything, but they wouldn't come."

"We chased after them, but the closer we got, the faster they went."

"Until they got to school here, and . . . well, you see what they did. They knocked over the set and the walls and . . . "

School?

"Don't worry," Mr. Monroe said, knocking water out of his ear, "we'll get the stage set up again in no time, and the play will go on as scheduled."

Mrs. Monroe turned to a woman standing next to her and said apologetically, "I'm sorry about your carrot cake. I'm sure it would have won first prize in the bake-off. It was so clever of you to bake it in the shape of a carrot and put that scrumptuous-looking cream-cheese frosting on it. I don't know what got into Chester."

"I don't know what got into Chester, Mom," said Pete, "but he sure got into that carrot cake." A chuckle ran through the crowd.

"And Harold's acting weird, too," Toby said.

"Well," said Mr. Monroe, "I can guess what happened with our friend Harold. He must've thought I was drowning and tried to save me. You can't expect a dog to understand things like a Dunk-the-Teacher booth at a school carnival."

Dunk-the-Teacher booth? Carnival? I thought. What's a carnival? I looked around me at the brightly colored streamers that festooned the school playground, the booths, the balloons, the clown who was at that moment walking by. So *this* is where everybody was headed! Zombies, indeed.

"I'd say you have *four* unusual pets," said a man in the crowd, tapping Mrs. Monroe on the shoulder. Mrs. Monroe just shook her head and sighed.

"Yes," someone else said, "maybe you should have entered them all in the pet contest."

Chester jumped down from Pete's arms and ran over to me. "That reminds me," he said, "we've got to find Bunnicula before he—"

Howie cut him off with a sharp yip. "Look," he cried, squirming out of Toby's armhold and jumping to the ground. "Over there on that table!"

We looked up and saw a cage made to look like a castle. "Castle Bunnicula" read a sign atop it. On the front was a big blue ribbon that proclaimed "First Prize—Most Unusual Pet in Centerville." And inside was none other than our long-lost furry friend . . . Bunnicula!

We scurried over to the rabbit's cage and peered in. He was sleeping soundly . . . the sleep, as they say, of the innocent.

"So that's where he's been," Howie whispered.

I glared at Chester. "Somebody goofed," I said. "If you don't deserve that prize, nobody does."

Chester yawned. Then he smiled weakly at Howie and me. "Well, boys," he said, "it's been quite a day, hasn't it?"

I was about to place my paws around his neck when Mrs. Monroe came up behind us.

"Phew, do you fellas smell!" she said. "Where have you been?"

It's a long story, I thought.

She called across the school playground to Mr. Monroe, who was on the platform helping some other people put the stage set back together.

"Robert!" she said, "I'm going to take these guys home and give them a quick bath. They smell as if they've been to the town dump. I'll be back as soon as I can."

"Hurry, Mom," Toby shouted. "I don't want you to miss the play."

We walked single-file behind Mrs. Monroe, our heads hanging, our tails drooping, all the way home.

"Well, Chester," I mumbled, "now that we've made total fools of ourselves, what do you have to say?"

"A slight misinterpretation of the facts," he replied. "Everyone's entitled to one slight misinterpretation of the facts in the course of a lifetime."

Suddenly, Howie said, "Psst, Uncle Harold, don't look now, but you're being watched."

I looked up and saw a large white cat hanging over the front porch railing of his home, his beady eyes following my every step. He hissed. I gulped.

"Remember me?" he said as I passed.

"Uh . . . well . . . uh . . . "

"Don't worry, buster," he went on, his eyes narrowing to slits. "You *will* remember me. One of these days, I'll give you something to remember me by."

I gulped again, wondering what it would be like never to leave home again.

"Don't worry, Uncle Harold," Howie said, apparently overhearing my throat muscles contract, "Snowball may or may not be serious in threatening you. After all, he could be just kitten."

I resisted the temptation to bounce Howie the rest of the way home.

"Ha ha ha," Howie chortled. "Get it, Uncle Harold? Just *kitten*! That's a cat joke. Wait'll I tell Pop. I'll knock him dead."

Or vice versa, I thought.

I sighed as I mulled over the possibilities fate held in store for me: captive forever in a house with wise-cracking Howie and adventure-loving Chester, with squabbling Toby and Pete and a television set that's possessed, or free in the world where Snowball was waiting to rearrange my body hair. How complicated life had become for a dog who wanted only the simple pleasures: peace and quiet and the occasional cream-filled chocolate cupcake.

I appreciated anew the old expression: it's a dog's life!

[EIGHT]

Home Is Where
the Heart Is

THAT EVENING, bathed, fed and re-
freshed, I felt life returning to a semblance
of normalcy. I was curled up on the rug contentedly chewing a recent copy of *Architectural Digest,* while nearby Howie and Chester were trying

to help Toby and Pete solve a Rubik's Cube. Howie's idea of helping was to grab it with his teeth and race to the other side of the room before the boys could get it away from him. Time after time they succeeded in retrieving it, however, until he finally tired of the game and began playing tug-of-war with Mr. Monroe's slipper. Unfortunately, Mr. Monroe's foot was still in residence in his slipper, so that didn't last long either. Bunnicula sat in his cage, staring out at the rest of us and twitching his nose, which I guess is a rabbit's way of having fun. Or at least passing the time. His First Prize ribbon adorned his regular cage; Castle Bunnicula, I gathered, having been relegated to the garage or one of the boy's bedrooms.

The *Architectural Digest* clamped in my jaws lost its interest when Mrs. Monroe appeared suddenly at the kitchen door carrying a plate of fudge. I ran to her side and begged shamelessly.

"Well, hello, Harold, what do you want?" she said. "This isn't dog food, you know."

It is to *this* dog, I thought.

Toby piped up, "He knows it's not dog food, Mom. Harold loves chocolate."

"Really? What makes you say that?"

I got a little nervous then, thinking that Toby was about to blow our late-night snack routine. I gave him a look, and he seemed to get the message.

"Oh, I don't know," he replied with a shrug. "He just . . . drools a lot . . . whenever I'm eating a candy bar. Why don't you give him a piece, and we'll find out if he likes it?" Toby winked at me.

"I don't know. It might be bad for him," Mrs. Monroe said. I gazed up at the plate in her hands with an expression of desire usually found only in the pages of novels with titles like *Wretched, Reckless Love* or *Forest Fire in the Timberland of My Heart*. Mrs. Monroe smiled down at me.

"Well, I guess one little piece of fudge once in a while never hurt anybody, now, did it?" She lowered a piece to my quivering lips, and I was in instant heaven.

The next hour or so passed peaceably enough as the Monroes recalled the day's events. Apparently, after our abrupt departure from the school carnival, everything had gone on as planned. *Curse of the Vampires,* though slightly delayed and redecorated (the portrait hanging on the wall was now of a man with a hole in his head), was a huge success. Mr. Monroe went back to his Dunk-the-Teacher booth where things went, you might say, swimmingly. And Mrs. Monroe's friend's carrot cake, the one Chester had demolished in his service to mankind, won first prize in the bake-off, the first time in culinary history a cake has won an award posthumously.

And now, we were all back home, safe and sound from our various adventures. Well, safe anyway. I'm not too sure how sound one could ever expect Chester to be.

Later that night, after everyone had gone to bed, he confided in me that he was still convinced Bunnicula had gotten loose and gone on a rampage throughout the town.

"Otherwise, how can you explain all those white vegetables? They had nothing to do with the school carnival," he said. "And where *was*

Bunnicula, anyway? We know he wasn't in his cage in the living room last night."

Howie dropped the bone he was carrying around the room and ran to Chester and me. "I just remembered something Pete said to Mr. Monroe tonight."

"What's that?" Chester asked.

"He said it had been a good idea to put Bunnicula in his new cage . . . you know, the Castle Bunnicula one they made for the carnival . . . so that he could get used to it. He spent the night in it in the garage."

"So there you are," I said. "He couldn't have gotten out. He was safe in the garage all night and . . ."

Suddenly, I gasped.

"What is it, Harold?" Chester asked.

"Mr. Monroe came running into the house this morning with the news that the garage door had been left open all night," I said. "So Bunnicula could have gotten out."

"And could have . . . in fact, *did* . . . turn all those vegetables white. Let's hope we got them all. Because it's night once again. Night. The time when the vampires come out to prey on the helpless, to attack, to drain their victims dry, to—"

"All right," I said, "enough. Let's not get into this nonsense about a bunch of silly vegetables."

"Th-that's r-r-right," Howie said, his teeth chattering, "because you're r-really scaring m-m-me."

"Let's get some sleep," I suggested. "It's been a long day."

"Good idea," Howie said. "Uncle Harold?"

"Yes, Howie?"

"Uh . . . may I curl up with you tonight? I'm a little nervous."

"Why, certainly," I replied. "As long as you have your pop's permission."

"Pop?"

Chester glared at both of us. "Spare me your feeble attempts at comedy, Harold. Good night."

"Good night," I said, stretching out on the rug. Howie rolled up into a little ball along my belly and in no time at all was fast asleep.

"Good night, Bunnicula," I called out softly.

Bunnicula blinked at me, a look of peace and contentment upon his face.

I was just about to drift off, when I noticed Chester sit up suddenly in the armchair he'd chosen for his night's slumber.

"What's that?" he cried in a whisper.

"What's what?" I asked.

"Coming from the floor . . . there, under the floorboards . . . I can hear it going 'thump, thump, thump' . . . Tear up the planks!"

"Have you lost your mind?" I said.

"It's coming from under the sofa." Chester jumped off the chair and dashed to the sofa. With his paw, he pulled back the dust ruffle and batted a white object out from underneath.

"Here, here!" he said. "It is the beating of this hideous heart!"

"Well, how'd that artichoke heart get there?" I asked. Then with a shrug I turned to Chester and said, "Come on, Chester, let's get some sleep."

"But, Harold, it's almost midnight. Who knows what evil lurks—"

"Cut it out, Chester. I want to sleep!"

And that's just what I set out to do when, moments later, I heard it.

"Thump . . . thump . . . thump . . ."

My ears perked up. One eye popped open, then the other. I regarded the object lying just inches away from my nose. Could it be? I wondered. No, it was just Chester's imagination.

"Thump . . . thump . . . thump . . ."

Still . . .

"Chester?" I whispered. My voice seemed to echo in the darkened room.

"Hmm?" Chester replied wearily.

"You wouldn't happen to have a toothpick, would you?"